No Ordinary Summer

TIFFANY LONETTO

PUBLISHED BY

SIGMA'S
BOOKSHELF

MINNETONKA, MN 55305
WWW.SIGMASBOOKSHELF.COM

No Ordinary Summer by Tiffany Lonetto

Copyright © 2018 by Sigma's Book Shelf.

Printed in the United States of America

First Printing 2018

ISBN 978-0-9996577-1-3

Chapter 1

Getting ready

As my perfume bottle rolled off the end of my bed to the floor I reached down to grab it. While doing so, I felt the small cardboard box under my bed filled with old family pictures. For some reason, I felt compelled to hop off the bed, sit down on the floor and look through the old pictures of my family happy, healthy, and together. As I did tears flowed down my cheeks.

My name is Carly Anderson. I am sixteen and what you would call the average teenager. I have long brown hair that I have been growing out since elementary school. My nickname is bug because when I was little I used to eat them for "protein" my mom would say. I wear leggings and oversized t-shirts almost every day because who has time to get ready?

When I was fourteen, my parents got divorced. My mom, whose name is Carrie Anderson, is a total control freak and thinks that she can fix everything, but she can't. When my little brother, Carson, was ten, he was diagnosed with stage IV lung cancer. My mom tried everything she could possibly do to cure Carson. When she realized that it was something she couldn't do, she went absolutely insane. My dad, whose name is Joe Anderson, couldn't deal with it, so he left her and took me and my two brothers with.

We moved to a run-down old apartment complex in Downtown Minneapolis. My mom moved down to Cocoa Beach, Florida to live her and my dad's dream on her own. My mom has not really been around to support or watch her kids grow, which has been tough on all of us, especially my dad. We have tried to get more involved with her by going to see her every summer in Cocoa Beach, which is where me and my brothers will fly to tomorrow.

As I continued packing, the smell of chicken and mashed potatoes made its way to my bedroom, so I went to see what was cooking. I walked into the dining room and found my brothers and dad sitting at the dinner table dishing up, so I joined them.

When we finished up eating and my brothers had both made their way to their rooms, I noticed my dad sniffing into the sleeve on his ripped sweatshirt as he scrubbed the dishes. I walked over to him and put my hand on his shoulder as he looked at me with watery eyes.

"What's wrong?" I asked him

"Every time you kids go to Cocoa Beach I fear you won't come back home," he said.

"Of course we will!" I said.

My dad should know he doesn't have to worry. We kids can hardly stand her for the summer as it is, but I guess it's just the thought that scares him. I comforted my dad with a big hug and assured him his greatest fear will never come true as we walked to our bedrooms to go to sleep.

* * *

The next morning I woke up to the smell of freshly cooked eggs and bacon. Knowing that is my brothers' favorite breakfast, I rushed to the door to beat them to the bacon so I would at least get a piece. My dad was already sitting at the table waiting to eat, and had bacon on his plate already, so he didn't need to worry.

"Good morning Dad," I said.

"Hi Carly. How are you doing this morning?" he asked.

"Okay I guess," I said, looking into his sad-looking brown eyes. Thinking he wanted me to say something more I added, "Just a bit anxious about the Florida trip."

"No need to be anxious," he said. "I know you'll have a good time."

After eating breakfast with my family, I excused myself to take a shower before going to hang out with my best friend and hot boyfriend. Me and Meghan have been best friends since kindergarten. Interestingly enough, our friendship began after she hit me in the face with a tiny plastic pan from our fake cooking class. After that incident, the teacher put us in a hoola hoop where we remained until we made up.

Me and Meghan are inseparable. She has been to every family gathering, every birthday party, and everything since then. Sometimes I think Meghan knows me better than I know myself which I know is kind of crazy, but it's true.

John, my smoking hot boyfriend, is the basic "captain/quarterback of the varsity football team type." We have been dating since seventh grade when we were crushing on each other and teasing each other about dating and getting married. Maybe we will someday. We have a wonderful relationship. I could never ever see myself functioning and living an everyday normal life without Meghan and John by my side! I love those two to death and that will never change.

Once I got out of the shower, I started to pack up the rest of my bathroom stuff before heading out to go meet my loves. There they sat waiting for me to roll up in my dad's Chevy truck. I got out and hugged them both and we headed into Megan's house to hangout and talk before I had to leave for Florida.

Saying goodbye to my best friend and the love of my life is something I dread doing every summer, but it's more of a "see you later" than a "goodbye". Meghan and John dread it just as much as I do. After four hours of laughing till we cried and talking until our mouths were sore, it was time to say "see you later." As I hugged Meghan to death, and kissed John to death, we said our "see you laters" and headed in different directions. I always get a little emotional when the time comes, but I know I'll see them again soon.

Chapter 2

The trip to Florida

"Carly, Carson, Casey, time to go," shouted Dad as he impatiently waited just outside the door for the three of us to come out. I guess you could say we were dragging our feet, but it was time.

"We're coming," I replied, then looked over at Carson and Casey and motioned for them to follow me. If they weren't five years apart, you'd think Carson and Casey were twins. They both are crazy about the game of football, and have the same sandy brown hair and brown eyes. Only, of course, Casey is taller because he is older.

With blank looks on our faces, all three of us made our way out the door. I locked it behind me, then followed my brothers to the truck. It's not necessarily a bad thing to be going to a mansion on the beach in Florida, but we all hate leaving Dad behind.

For the most part, we stayed silent during the entire half-hour-long drive to the airport. When we got to there, Dad parked in the short-term parking lot, then hopped into the truck bed to grab our bags. He handed them to each of us, then we headed inside. My brothers managed their own bags just fine, but my dad had to help me with mine because what girl doesn't pack her whole room when she goes somewhere?

Once inside, we had to stand in a long line to drop off our bags. Carson stood in line for a few minutes, but when it became obvious he was getting tired of standing Dad said, "Hey buddy. Come over here and let me hold you for a bit." Carson reached up and let Dad grab him, then put his head on Dad's shoulder.

When we finally reached the front of the line, we handed our bags over to the Delta Air Lines employees and made our way over to our flight gate where we sat and waited. Fortunately because we are unaccompanied minors, our dad was allowed to come to the gate with us. Usually only ticketed passengers are allowed to go down to the gate.

Once we sat down, Casey finally broke his silence and said, "Why are you making us go see her? You know I hate going to Florida! It's not fair!"

"Casey, we've been through this before. Your mother has partial custody of you kids and our divorce agreement says she gets custody of you three in the summertime and for every other Christmas. Next year when you turn eighteen you can make up your own mind about whether you want to spend time with her or not, but for now you're under court order to do so," said Dad.

"I like visiting Florida, especially Disney World," said Carson, surprising all of us. He usually doesn't speak up when Casey gets into one of his moods.

"I like going to Florida too," I said, trying to offer Carson some comfort.

I wasn't sure where the conversation was going to go next, but didn't have to worry about it because just then a voice came over the intercom and said, "Attention passengers traveling on Flight 2122 to Orlando, Florida. Boarding is about to begin.

We hugged Dad and said our goodbyes, then got into line to board the plane. I turned back every so often as we made our way towards the boarding tunnel, and he was still there. I blew him a kiss before leaving his sight, and he did the same.

Once we got on the plane, it didn't take long to find our seats in First Class. I sat in the middle, between my two brothers. Once all the passengers were onboard, we listened to the boring flight attendant go over the safety rules and explain what to do if we were to crash. I had heard it all before, so I just put my headphones on to block what she was saying out. I started to doze off after the plane took off.

I woke up about an hour and a half into the flight to see my brothers passed out on both sides of me, so I went back to sleep. Another hour and a half or so passed before I was awakened by Carson shaking me as the plane was starting to tilt down. "Carly, Carly, time to wake up. We're almost there," he said.

"Okay, okay," I responded, realizing it was time to land. As the tires set down, I was thankful that the flight was good and safe because you know... everyone has that fear in the back of their mind that something might go wrong every time they fly.

Chapter 3

Greetings

After getting off the plane, we made our way to baggage claim to get our stuff. When we arrived, we were greeted by a sign held in the air that said, "Anderson Family." Holding it was Edwin, the funniest, most caring butler I have ever met. Edwin already had our luggage around him when we ran up to give him a hug. He was just as happy to see us as we were him.

"Edwin, Edwin, we're here," shouted Carson.

"Hey there little man," he said scooping Carson up in his arms. "It is so good to see you, Carly, and Casey. I have missed you guys!"

Edwin is about six-foot-two, has brown hair, and a dashing smile. Edwin has been around my family since I was about five years old. He used to work at a restaurant my family would go to every time we came to Florida together. Edwin started helping my mom out when she moved down to Florida by herself. He then started going grocery shopping, and cleaning her house daily. My mom then had Edwin quit his job and start working for her. He has been there for us ever since.

After getting the greetings out of the way, we followed Edwin to the limo. Yes, my mom has a butler who gets driven around in a limo. If I haven't mentioned it yet, my mom has money. A great amount of it. She is very wealthy and living her life alone just fine. That is except for the fact that my mom tends to drink a lot. At least she has been since we got the news about Carson. She turned to alcohol instead of her family, which is how she went downhill. She hasn't stopped drinking since she left Minnesota. I don't know how she manages to run her company, Carrie's Clothing (CC), which is the biggest clothing design firm in the State of Florida.

As we drove through the gates at the beginning of her half a mile-long driveway, Carson looked at me and smiled nervously. Then he looked up at our mother standing on the deck in the front of her three-story white house full of windows, and frowned. As the car came to a stop, she came down the stairs to greet us all and help carry in our bags.

Now if it was Dad we were greeting, all of us would have run right up to him and given him a giant bear hug, but this is Mom we were talking about. We all just kind of stood there. "Hi kids," she said, breaking the silence. "It is so great to see you all!"

I hate to say it, but her words didn't exude warmth. She appeared happy to see us, as she was smiling, but she too was just standing there. You'd think a mother would run over to her kids and hug them after having not seen them for a long time, but she did nothing of the sort.

Interestingly, it was Carson who made the first move. "Hello Mother! It is nice to see you."

"Yeah, nice," I said.

"Nice," agreed Casey.

Once we got the greetings out of the way, we made our way into Mom's million-dollar home. She just stood at the bottom of the stairs as I followed Carson to his room to help him unpack. You'd think she'd want to follow us up

or something, but no, she didn't. I could tell Carson was
not too happy about that.

He is usually weird and a little bit off for a few days after
leaving my dad. He is not very fond of my mother, being
that she left him when he needed her the most. My dad has
always been there for us. My dad is very close with every one
of us, especially Carson since we found out the news. I am
not sure which family member was most affected by Carson's diagnosis. My mom wanted to help but couldn't. My
dad and Casey were both more closed off, and pretty closed
off from everyone else. They went into a deep depression
I guess you could call it, but eventually got better. Carson
mostly acted like nothing ever happened and he wasn't sick
to keep up everyone's mood in the family.

After helping Carson unpack, I made my way back down-
stairs. I was kind of hoping I'd run into Mom, but I didn't,
so I went out to the yurt in the backyard to unpack my
five different suitcases and make it look like my room again.
I first opened the two back doors, then walked out onto
the balcony. My room is right on the shore of the ocean. It
has a bathroom so I don't have to go back into the house
every time I have to go. It is basically a huge room with an
attached bathroom seven feet above the shore line of the
ocean. My mom used it as a craft room when she felt artsy,
but she fell out of that phase way too quick and turned
it into a guest room. Me and Casey switch every other
summer for who gets it as their awesome room. Really the
only reason he likes it is so if he finds a random girl from
the ocean or streets he can bring her over without going
through Mom and Edwin to do it.

That girl off the streets half the time happens to be Lucy,
the worst girl of all. She is that basic white girl who thinks
she's better than everyone else and thinks she knows everything. Casey has Lucy wrapped around his fingers and you

all know what for... gross. Casey is the oldest. He is a year older than me. He and my boyfriend, John, just graduated this last school year.

He and John get along actually pretty well when a PlayStation 4 is involved. Casey is my dad's best friend and a pretty rotten but loving brother if you know what I mean. He is spoiled like the rest of us, and is actually not too bad looking, so he is a total ladies' man.

Anyway, after I finished unpacking, I went outside to sit on the balcony. I was dangling my feet over the ledge, just admiring the view of the colorful clouds hanging over the sky blue transparent ocean water when I heard loud stomping feet coming up the stairs.

"Hi Carly, I'm guessing that since you're out here you're done unpacking," said Casey as he sat down next to me.

"Yeah, I'm done," I said.

"I am too," said Carson, out of breath as he came running up the stairs behind Casey and sat down next to both of us.

Before long we were all dangling our legs over the ledge as we talked about the beautiful view, and the move for the summer in general. We stopped to listen as we heard more footsteps come closer. It was my mom. She had come to tell us it was time to start getting ready for dinner. We were going to the biggest, most popular Italian restaurant in the whole state of Florida and had to change into nicer clothes.

Carson and Casey ran back down the stairs followed by Mom, who still hadn't really attempted any kind of conversation with me. Oh well, I thought. I then went back into the yurt and put my soft, white, dress on, then threw a few curls in my hair along with some mascara on my eyelashes. I then headed down the stairs and slowly made my way towards the house. Nothing is better than the feeling of the soft, warm sand underneath your feet.

Chapter 4

Quite the night

As we hopped into the limo and headed to the restaurant, Mom and Edwin asked about the school year and how it was going. Carson talked excitedly about all the cool things his fourth grade teacher had done that year, and showed off how he knew his states in alphabetical order. Oh good, I thought, he'll keep them entertained the whole way there.

I pulled my iPhone out of my bag and threw a text at Dad, John and Meghan about how the flight went and what we were heading to do right now. I miss them all so much already.

When we arrived at the restaurant, cameras were flashing everywhere. When Edwin opened the door, people went crazy as my mom stepped out and smiled and waved like she's some kind of Kardashian or something. "Hello," she shouted over and over again, as she waved to the reporters.

Nobody was really paying attention to me when I stepped out of the limo with my brothers. No, they were all snapping pictures of my mom as she made her way into the restaurant. It's a good thing nobody captured the look on my face when I spotted the enemy, Lucy, standing next to her mom, the owner of the second biggest clothing line in the State of Florida. I'm sure my evil eye would have gotten Mom some negative attention, which would not have gone over very well.

By the way, Lucy's hatred for my mom is unreal. Her mom, Lee, is nothing when my mom is around. Lee and Lucy can't stand playing second fiddle to her. The hate between me and Lucy began when she tried to date my brother, Casey, to get at my mom for her mom, ridiculous.

When we walked into the restaurant, we were quickly seated. "What took you so long?" asked Mom.

"We got stuck behind all the camera people," I said.

"I didn't know you were a movie star," added Carson.

"No sweetie, just a well-known clothing designer," said Mom, who snapped her fingers to call over a passing waiter so she could order a drink. There were celebrities everywhere eating dinner like it was nothing. It's nothing to my mom either.

Dinner was going well until my mom started getting drunk. I mean what did she expect after ordering at least five drinks in the matter of an hour? When she started slurring her words and laughing at everything, Edwin knew it was time to cut the evening short and go home. We had barely finished dinner, and didn't even get a chance to look at the desert menu, not that any of us wanted to stick around. Mom's behavior was embarrassing to all three of us.

She actually passed out in the car on the way home. Unreal!

When we arrived back home, everyone went to their separate rooms. I changed out of my dressy clothes and put on sweatpants and pajamas, then hopped into bed with my cell phone. My first call was to John, then Meghan and finally my dad. After about an hour of talking, I slowly fall asleep.

At exactly 2:06 a.m., I woke up to the sounds of my

mom screaming and crying, then the words finally registered. "Something is wrong with Carson! Come back into the house, quick!"

I woke up to her grabbing and pulling me out of bed. I rubbed my eyes as I threw off the covers, then got up and ran down the stairs and over to the house. I found Carson curled up in a ball in Casey's arms. He was screaming and crying in pain.

As soon as he spotted me, Carson reached out to me, tried to smile and softly said, "Carly." I was in tears when I picked him up and screamed at Edwin to call 9-1-1. I rocked Carson back and forth in my arms for only a few moments before hearing the sirens come closer and closer to us. Moments later, the first responders took Carson from my arms and strapped him on the stretcher. I followed them into the back of the ambulance, and watched the doors close, then looked over at my little brother. His face was white and his eyes were closed as the motor started up and the vehicle pulled away. I could hear the sirens and thought they would have been louder, but they seemed kind of distant, as if blaring in a dream rather than for real.

Chapter 5

Nightmare to reality

When we arrived at the E.R., there was a whole team of medical people waiting. They transferred Carson onto a hospital cart, then wheeled him to a room to get settled in and hooked up to IVs. I have never been as scared or upset as I am right now. Carson looked at me with watery eyes as they gave him shots of pain medicine. He made solid eye contact with me for every shot he got, as I struggled to keep myself together. Once the pain had finally subsided, he closed his eyes and I reached for his hand.

When my mom and Casey showed up a few minutes later, they found me lying next to Carson in the hospital bed. He was asleep with a peaceful look on his face. I, on the other hand, was a mess. "How's he doing?" asked my mom, barely holding back the tears.

"I don't know," I said, tearing up again. "He hasn't said anything to me since he called out my name at the house."

"I talked to the doctor and they are going to run some tests," said Mom. "They're just waiting for a call from his doctor up in Minnesota before getting started."

Mom sat down on the bed next to us and grabbed Carson's other hand. Casey pulled up a chair and sat down nearby. We all sat silently just staring at Carson for about ten minutes, and then the techs came to take him to get a PET scan, which is the tool they use to see the cancer in Carson's lungs. As he was being wheeled away, I walked out into the hallway to call my dad and let him know what was happening, and everything that had just gone down. By the time I got off the phone with my dad I was so upset I needed to take a moment to get myself back together before I went to see Carson. He had just gotten back from the scan.

When I walked into the room, I sat on the end of the bed and put my hand on his knee. He looked up at me, smiled, and then said, "Carly, I am okay now. The doctors are going to help me."

I nodded my head up and down at Carson because I couldn't find the words to say. I looked down as the doctor walked into the room. He slid the glass door quietly behind him. I knew I wasn't ready for what was about to be said, but I had to be. He then walked over to my mom where he rested his hand on hers, then handed her a picture, a picture of Carson's body. My mom then burst into tears and dropped the picture on the ground. I glanced down at it and saw that Carson's body was lit up like a Christmas tree. He was full of cancer. I slowly closed my eyes as the tears started streaming down my cheeks.

Casey then stormed out of the room. As he left he pushed a cart full of medicine over, and kicked a small garbage can across the hallway. He then fell to his knees in the middle of the hall and started wailing. My mom rushed over to grab hold of Casey before the security guards could and brought him out to the lobby. The doctor then put his hand on my shoulder and asked me to join him out in the hallway. Before I left the room, I kissed Carson on the forehead. He smiled at me.

"I'll be right back buddy," I told him, and he nodded. I then followed the doctor out into the hall. He shut the door behind us, then began to tell me something that sent chills down my spine, and a stabbing pain into my heart.

The doctor told me that Carson has a matter of one-to-five months to live the rest of his life. Apparently, chemotherapy is no match for the amount of cancer in his twelve-year-old body. "There's really not much more we can do now than keep him comfortable," he said.

As the doctor told me more and more, I zoned him out. I leaned on the glass door, looked in, and saw Carson, an innocent twelve-year-old boy, resting his eyes. A boy who has to suffer for the last one-to-five months of life he has. The doctor then patted my shoulder and moved on to his next patient down the hall.

I turned around and saw Casey and my mom staring at me. They had heard the whole conversation. "I am so sorry," said Casey as he came over and hugged me.

"Me too," I stuttered as the tears started flowing again. We both cried our eyes out that night.

Sitting in the lobby with Mom and Casey, who was trying to get some sleep, I stared at the ceiling, thinking how could this happen? How could this disease take over a whole body and why my little brother's to be exact? He doesn't deserve this!

I must have eventually fallen asleep because the next thing I knew there was sunshine beating into my eyes. I looked over to see my mom on the phone and Casey sipping on a hot chocolate, as he handed me one. We walked back to Carson's room and he had a big grin on his face. You could tell he was as excited to us as we were to see him. The doctor then came in and told us that Carson could be released from the hospital today, and will just be sent home with shots of pain meds so he can live pain free for as long as he has.

As the reality hit that my brother has just a limited amount of time left to live his life, I pledged to do everything in my power to make him as comfortable as humanly possible. When he came home, I helped him set up his room to make it look exactly the way he wanted it. Once he was all comfy and cozy in his room, I went out to mine. When I got out to my room, I shut the door behind me, then I fell apart. I felt so helpless and worthless. I wasn't sure what to do next. I knew I couldn't show fear or Carson would be even more scared than he already is. I put myself back together and walked out to my usual hanging-out spot on the balcony, and hung my feet above the shore line.

I then heard footsteps. There was Carson, limping up the stairs towards the yurt. When he reached the top of the stairs, he plopped down next to me. "Sorry I scared you at the hospital last night," he said with genuine concern on his face.

I didn't know what to say, so I didn't say anything. He then asked me if he is going to be okay. As I looked into Carson's light blue eyes, I felt a tear slip from mine. "Yes, it is going to be okay," I told him, while running my fingers through his dark brown hair. Carson then proceeded to tell me he heard the whole conversation between me and the doctor.

"Carly, I know I don't have much time left, but it's going to be okay," he said. I grabbed hold of him and hugged him tight. With my chin resting on his head, I said, "We are going to make the next couple of months the best months ever!"

He smiled and shook his head in agreement. We then headed back to the house to make ourselves some macaroni and cheese. After we finished eating, I followed Carson into his room so he could lay down to rest. His medicine makes him very drowsy, which is a sucky side effect, but it is better than being in pain.

Chapter 6

Before I die

As I watched Carson fall into a deep, dreamy sleep, I decided to head back to my own bed. As I was hopping off his bed, I looked down and saw something on the floor. It was a crumpled-up ball of notebook paper. I opened it up and recognized Carson's handwriting. The writing on the paper said, "Before I die list." A tear of mine splashed down onto the paper. I then proceed to read it.

Learn to surf
Dinner at the beach
Watch the sun rise over the ocean
Make a car out of Legos
Swim with dolphins
Fight for my life

As I slowly backed out of his room and shut the door quietly behind me, I saw my mom stumbling into her bedroom, drunker than a skunk and in tears. I shook my head, not so much in disbelief, but disappointment. Just then, Edwin came up to me with a bowl of my favorite kind of ice cream. He handed me the bowl and said, "Here, you need it."

I grinned at Edwin and said, "Thanks!"

We sat together at the dining room table for the next several hours, venting about this whole ordeal and discussing how we can make the wishes on Carson's list come true. As Edwin's head started to bob at the table, we knew it was time to call it a night. We both headed to our rooms.

I plopped down on my bed and grabbed my cell phone off the nightstand. I haven't been on it in at least two days. There were an insane amount of text messages and missed calls on it from Dad, John, and Meg. I called Dad and could hear the depression and sadness in his voice, which was raspy. He tried to act tough, but I could tell he had been crying. Dad told me he would soon be coming down to Florida for the rest of the summer, and would be living just two miles away from my mom's house in their old condo. They used to rent it out, but fortunately there aren't any tenants in it currently. He planned to arrive in less than a week! He told me that he needs a vacation and needs to be with Carson. We can't risk flying Carson back to Minnesota in his condition, so Dad is coming to Florida

It looked like we were going to be in Florida for a little bit longer than we expected. When I got off the phone with my dad, I called Meghan then added John to the phone call as I vented to them about the situation.

"It's not fair!" I cried out over and over again during that call. "It's just not fair!"

I eventually fell asleep with them over the phone.

When I woke up, I headed into the house to eat the breakfast that Edwin had made for us. Waiting for me were freshly cut fruits and fresh waffles, yum!

When I walked into the breakfast nook, Carson and Casey were already at the table and I slammed the crumpled-up paper on the table in front of Carson for effect.

"Are you ready young man?" I asked.

"Ready for what?" asked Carson.

"Ready to make the dreams on that piece of paper come true?"

"Oh that," he whispered with an embarrassed look on his face. "Nobody was supposed to see that."

"Well I did, and now we're going to do what's on that list. Ready to find out how well a car made out of Legos can drive?"

Carson's face lit up with the biggest smile I've ever seen him show. I told him to meet me by the car. Mom winked at Carson as she handed me her credit card. "Now go out and have a great time," she told us.

Not ten minutes later, I was sitting in the driver's seat waiting, then I saw Casey come running my way with Carson on his back. "Are you ready for an ad-ven-ture?" shouted Casey as he deposited Carson in the back seat, then closed the back door and slid in next to me. We then drove into town, screaming at the top of our lungs to the old Miley Cyrus songs, as I moved my hips like yeah to "Party in the USA."

We parked at the nearest toy shop, then raced in to find every different color and sticker available for Legos. "Carly, Carly over here. Look at these cool Lego guys. Wouldn't they look neat sitting on the hood?"

"Sure, grab a handful," said Casey, and he did. An hour or so later we all walked out with our hands full of bags that contained over $5,000 worth of Legos. On the way home from the toy store we talked about how we would go about building Carson's car. When we got home, we rushed into the house with the bags of Legos in our hands, and cleared out the living room.

"Carson, help me stack the chairs," I said after Casey and I had moved the heavy table to the corner of the room. We then started unpacking and building the Legos.

We worked feverishly for two hours straight, that is until Edwin walked over with three grilled cheese sandwiches. "Hey guys, you're working so hard you must be hungry by now," he said, as he set them down on the table.

"We can't stop now," said Carson, as he ran over to the table to grab half a sandwich, then rushed back over to his new car under construction. Casey and I copied Carson, and grabbed our sandwiches off the table, gobbling them down as we worked. Edwin smiled and left us to it.

With the three of us working nonstop, we continued to make more and more progress. Within three hours of working pretty much with no breaks, we had made a miniature car with tiny wheels that could move. When the car was just big enough to fit Carson's little body inside, he crawled inside and waited for Casey to give him a little push.

"There they go!" I said, as Carson got pushed around the living room by Casey. Eventually, Casey let go and Carson held on tight as the wheels turned on their own and the car eventually crashed into the wall. Edwin, me and Casey all held our breath, waiting for Carson's reaction.

He turned around and looked at us with a big grin before he burst out laughing along with the rest of us. Edwin then grabbed a pen to go check the item, "Make a car out of Legos," off Carson's list that was hanging on the fridge. When we all started to calm down from laughing so hard, Mom happened to walk in. As she looked around and noticed the little scratch on the wall from where Carson had crashed, she just laughed.

We then started to tell her the story of Carson's first driving adventure and laughed with her.

Chapter 7

Happiness

The night couldn't get any better, we thought, until Mom told us she had decided to seek therapy for her drinking problem. As she gave all us kids a hug, Edwin snapped a Polaroid, which I was going to treasure for a long time.

The night went on, and our entire family, minus Dad who had not arrived yet, binge-watched every Disney movie on Netflix. We ate popcorn until we couldn't keep our eyes open any longer, then all went off to our rooms to go sleep around 1 a.m.

The next day, Carson would learn to surf. I have been surfing since I was five years old. Edwin taught me how to surf because when he was a teenager he was in tons of different surfing competitions, and knew all the moves. He was a pro. Carson had always mentioned that he wanted to learn how to surf. He had watched me and Casey surf since he was just a baby, sitting on the beach with my mom.

I guess you could say Carson has had an obsession with the ocean since he was a little boy. Not only does he love being in and around the water, he has a huge obsession with dolphins. Why? No idea, but as soon as he found out what a dolphin was, and what one looked like, he was hooked. He is in love with dolphins and everything about them. He says that is a main reason he wants to surf. Because he feels as if he is a dolphin when he is gliding through the water. I sure hope we see one tomorrow when we take him surfing. That would really be exciting for him.

The next morning got started early for me. When I woke up I went down to the water to check the conditions and was delighted that the waves were kicking up a bit. I went bursting into the house to get Carson up, and found he and Casey playing the PlayStation in the living room.

"Time to get your swim trunks on Carson. Surf's up and we need to hang ten," I said.

"Oh yeah," he squealed. "Let me get my swim trunks on."

Carson dropped the PlayStation controller and ran to his room to change. Casey went the other way to the bathroom to change. Since I was already in my wetsuit with my bikini underneath, I headed out to the beach to start waxing up the surfboards. I grabbed my dad's old surfboard, the one he bought for himself when they would come to visit in the condo back when my parents were married. I knew it would be perfect for Carson to use.

"Carly, Carly, I'm ready," Carson shouted as he came running towards me. Casey was right behind him. I held up Dad's surfboard and when Carson saw it he stopped dead in his tracks and jumped for joy, then continued running towards me in excitement.

"Okay, hop on," I said to Carson, once the water around us was deep enough. Carson hopped onto the board. Casey and I each grabbed one side of it to keep it stable, and went out a bit farther, until the water was just above me and Casey's waists.

"Okay, now slowly get up and stand," I told Carson.

Small waves started breaking over the board as Carson built up enough strength to stand up and balance. Once he was up, me and Casey let go, and he floated to the next wave about a foot away from us. Then another wave came and he moved again, all on his own.

"Yeah Carson!" Mom and Edwin were cheering and jumping on shore with the camera in hand. Me and Casey started cheering as well, as he went over one more wave, then fell into the water. A second or two later, Carson popped up out of the water, laughing and throwing his hands in the air as we came over to help.

"Let's do that again!" he said.

"Okay. How about we launch you from over there this time," I said, pointing to a spot just past some rocks in the distance where the waves were breaking a bit stronger.

"Excellent!" shouted Carson, playing the part of the surfer dude.

We finally called it a day around dinner time. Until the sun had started getting lower in the sky, none of us realized we had missed lunch. We were all so determined. We discussed the day over dinner, then headed to our respective beds, as we were all so exhausted from being in the sun all day. I fell asleep while on the phone with Meg and John again.

The next morning, I woke up to Carson shaking me. "It's time to go surfing again, Carly, wake up please," he said.

I got up and got changed, then right after breakfast the three of us headed out to the ocean again, and did the same thing we had done he day before. Carson could only get over one wave at a time on his own, but that was okay. He wasn't training for a competition or anything. He was just out there having fun.

Chapter 8

Determined

As the end of the second day of surfing came along, Carson did it. He went over an even bigger wave than he had been practicing on, and on his own! Carson was determined that before he went in that night that he would be able to surf on the little waves on his own, and that he did. That day Carson could master little waves on his own and we were all so proud!

Carson had his own cheering session. Every time he surfed over a wave, at least one of us cheered so loudly other people on the beach must have thought we were crazy.

The last thing that happened that day was a good old fashioned water fight. It started at the water's edge with Carson running towards me at full speed, dragging the surfboard behind him. He took me out with a huge hug. We both fell down and went underwater, and as he came up got splashed by Casey. We splashed back, and eventually Mom and Edwin joined in the splash fight. Mom wasn't even in her bathing suit. She had on a sundress. We all splashed and laughed until the sun went down. Best night ever!

As I lay in my bed, I thought about the next day. The day when my dad would be coming down from Minnesota. Everyone was excited, including my mom, I think. Waking up the next morning, something felt different. I felt accomplished and beyond happy. Maybe today would be the day my family starts getting along again. Maybe everything would turn out alright.

As we headed to the airport, us kids were all excited, and Mom came with! When we found Dad sitting on the bench outside the airport with his phone up in the air, we couldn't tell if he trying to get a picture of the massive palm tree in front of him or trying to find service! Before any of us could say anything, he turned around to see his family and Edwin standing there, got up and ran over to Carson. They gave each other the biggest hug. Eventually, we all joined in, even Mom.

On the way back to the house, we shared with Dad all that has happened since we arrived in Florida. Carson couldn't stop smiling as he told Dad all about his surfing adventure. "Just wait till you see me up on the board," he said.

"Can't wait!" replied Dad.

After about an hour on the road, we rolled up to the condo Dad will be staying in. He had accepted Mom's invitation to go to a fashion show involving her company that evening, and needed to get ready.

He said goodbye, as he went inside to unpack and get ready. He had told us he'd take an Uber over to Mom's in about an hour. The hour passed quickly, and when Dad arrived at the house, he was dressed to kill. I always thought he looked good in a tuxedo.

When Mom came down the stairs wearing a designer dress of her own, the look on Dad's face was priceless. Same could be said about Mom's.

"Okay guys, time for you to get ready now," she said as she handed me a dress and tuxes to both of the boys. Our first event as a family in a long time was going to be watching her designer dresses get flaunted and shown off on a stage by ladies with size zero waists.

***

As I walked in behind my mother with my brothers and Dad, lights were flashing and flashing all around us. People were grabbing at my sleek, sheer red dress and asking if I was going to model for my mother. I have to admit I have thought about it, but being that I live in Minnesota, I wouldn't make many of the shows.

As me and my family rook our seats, my mom's phenomenal clothes came down the runway. I felt someone brush my shoulder, turned, and there she was. My nemesis, Lucy. She leaned forward to talk in my ear, and began the conversation by saying, "Since your brother is about to die, do you think your mom will lose her business and my mom can finally get the spot she deserves?"

I felt the blood in my body start to heat up, took a deep breath, then snatched her hair and pulled her forward to talk in her ear. "Keep talking the way you are, and he will live longer than you," I sneered. I let go and she flew back to her seat with a little squeal. Casey started laughing, then turned around to give a smart grin. When she saw that, Lucy crossed her arms in disgust.

When the show came to an end, we made our way to the reception room, where Mom would remain for the rest of the evening with Dad by her side.

Later that night, Mom and us kids we took a taxi back to the house, and Dad took an Uber to the condo. When we got home, I told my mom what Lucy had said to me, and what I said back, hoping that she wouldn't be mad that I threatened the daughter of her biggest competitor.

"Mad?" she asked, laughing. "No, not mad. Proud maybe,

but not mad."

I relaxed as Mom shook her head slightly before putting one hand up high for a high five.

"High five!" I said as we hugged goodnight. Then I headed out to my room.

Chapter 9

The List Continues

The next day Dad came over to Mom's, and my whole family hung out on the beach and surfed the day away. Carson was so excited to finally be able to surf with Dad. I think he was pretty impressed that I had managed to teach my little brother how to hang ten.

When the sun went down, and it started to get darker, everyone but me and Edwin made their way into the house. Mom, Dad and Casey were put in charge of distracting Carson while we worked on another item on Carson's list, namely dinner at the beach.

I set up a table with two small light poles on each side about eight feet out from the house. When everything was ready, I poked my head inside and shouted, "Carson, Casey, Mom and Dad, your presence is requested in the backyard."

I winked at Edwin, as we had been planning this for the past few days. Edwin had made delicious steaks with mashed potatoes and green beans. Carson led the way, as the entire family made its way out to the beach and sat down at the table set up by the water. The scene was perfect. As the ocean water quietly pounded the shore, my family took their places at the table. I went back inside to help Edwin bring out the food. As we all sat and ate and talked, Mom and Dad brought up old memories.

Joe chuckled, "Carrie, do you remember the time we brought Carly out to the water for the first time, and every time we took her out of it, she would cry and cry?"

"Oh my gosh, yes that was funny, but crazy at the same time," said Mom as she laughed.

They were both smiling more than I have ever seen before. Maybe this really is it. Maybe they will get back together soon. At least I hope they will.

By the end of dinner, the sky filled with color as we all sat on the shoreline with our toes in the sand. Mom was leaning on Dad's shoulder. Meantime, me, Edwin and my brothers had a back-rub line going.

When it started to get too dark to really see anymore, the adults decided to call it a night. "Why don't you kids camp out in the yurt tonight?" suggested Dad.

"Okay," said Casey, who winked at me. We both realized that meant Dad would probably be spending the night. That evening, me, Carson and Casey sat in the yurt playing Fortnite on the PlayStation 4 until we couldn't keep our eyes open anymore. The boys shared the bed and I fell asleep on the futon in the corner of the room.

The next morning we were awakened by the seagulls making a racket as they flew overhead. We headed out to the balcony just as the sun started to peek back over the ocean. Slowly but surely, we watched the sun make its way into the sky to light the beautiful Saturday. As we rushed back into the main house to cross off two more items on the list, Casey stopped dead in his tracks.

"Ouch, that hurt," he said as me and Carson slammed into the back of him.

"Sorry," I said. "Why did you stop so suddenly?"

"Look," he said, pointing at an amazing sight beyond the

sliding glass door. We saw Mom and Dad give each other a little peck on the cheek.

Carson looked over at me with a huge grin on his face, then opened the door. Mom jumped off the couch. Dad stood up too.

"Hi there kids," said Dad, who went on to explain that he and Mom had a long talk that evening and have decided to get back together.

"We still love each other, and of course all of you too," said Mom.

"Now come on over here and give us a hug," said Dad. Us kids gathered around for a group hug. I glanced into the kitchen and met eyes with Edwin. He grinned and raised an eyebrow, then invited us all to breakfast.

Once Mom and Dad started getting along so much better, it made everyone in the family happy. Every family member we had from both my mom's and dad's side were overjoyed at the thought of my parents getting back together. They have become the couple that everyone enjoys being around. It's so nice to see them happy again!

My fondest memories of this time in my life are going to be of Mom and Dad talking and sharing their old memories, starting from back when they were holding Casey, my seventeen-year-old model brother, in their arms for the first time all the way to just a few days ago when we picked Dad up at the airport. You could definitely tell that Mom and Dad missed each other and every little moment they weren't together in between. Mom and Dad were one of those couples everyone wanted to be. They could both be models even at the age they are now. They both have beautiful bright, blue eyes that they passed on to us three kids. Everyone asks if we kids will be models when we get older. Not to brag or anything, but in my opinion, I think we have a pretty good-looking family.

The last check box on Carson's list had yet to be checked off. Tomorrow we will be heading to Sea World's Discovery Cove, where Carson and the family will get the exciting opportunity to swim with dolphins.

Chapter 10

Fascinating

"Hurry, hurry, I don't want to be late," said Carson, as he ran out the front door. I guess the rest of us were moving too slow for him on what he had started referring to as the best day of his life. We were going to Sea World's Discovery Cove to swim with the dolphins.

After we all had piled into the limo, I started quizzing Carson on everything I knew about dolphins, and was impressed with his answers. "How many species of dolphins are there?" I asked.

"There are forty species of dolphins in the world," he said.

"Are dolphins fish or whales?"

"Whales!" he shouted.

"How many dolphins can live in a pod?"

"One-thousand," said Carson.

The question-and-answer session continued pretty much the entire way to Sea World. When we got there, the first thing we did was park up front in the handicapped parking area, and get Carson's wheelchair out of the back of the car.

"I don't want to ride. I want to run," said Carson, who got into the stance of a sprinter.

"Whoa, slow down Carson," said Dad, as he lifted him

up into the air, then set him down in his wheelchair. "You need to save your strength for the dolphin experience."

"Oh yeah, okay," he said, giving in quickly and sitting back in his wheelchair. We then made our way to the check-in area where there was a lot of activity underway. There were little kids running around, people wearing snorkels and masks popping in and out of the water, and of course dolphins swimming around in the lagoon.

When we came up to the water's edge, Dad reached for Carson's hand and then Mom's. I grabbed Carson's other hand and Casey's. My family stood there together very still until we heard someone shout, "Andersons, you're up."

We made our way towards the entry gate that led to the lagoon. As we were getting help putting our life jackets on, we watched these dolphins swim around. As we entered the water, sea turtles and dolphins were swimming all around us. Carson walked right out to the middle of the shallow pool. As he reached down, a dolphin popped its head out of the water and came face-to- face with Carson who squealed with delight. It was likely they had some sort of connection right off the bat.

The lady who works there then came over to Carson and asked, "Which dolphin do you want to swim with for the day?" she asked,

"The one that just came right up to me," he said pointing. "That one over there." The lady then blew her whistle and the dolphin Carson had been pointing at zipped underwater right over to him. The dolphin sat there like before as the lady started telling us about her.

"This is our oldest dolphin in the exhibit. Her name is Hope and she is thirty seven years old. Most dolphins grow to stretch up to forty inches," she said, then went on to tell Carson that every dolphin in the exhibit has its own quote based off its name. "Hope's quote is to 'never lose hope.'"

After she said that, Mom, Dad, Casey, and I teared up. Carson had tears in his eyes too. Not tears of sadness though. They were tears of pure joy and happiness, of course. I stood there wondering how in the world did Carson make a connection with a perfect dolphin and quote for him and his journey?

The lady then set each of us up with our own personal dolphins. We were instructed to hold onto their fins, then they pulled each of us around the lagoon like it was nothing. As I looked down, I spotted several sea turtles and fish swimming along with us. The non-working dolphins decided to join the party too. The whole experience was almost like a dream.

After three glorious hours of swimming with the dolphins, it was time to head out. "Thank you for coming. I hope you'll come again," said the lady as we were packing up to leave.

When we were going through the turnstiles, we all turned back to the lagoon and observed several dolphins jump up and down out of the water over and over again. They actually flapped their fins, as if they were waving goodbye.

"Bye guys," shouted Carson in their direction. "Thank you for a great day!"

"You're very welcome young man said our dolphin swimming instructor. We said our goodbyes and thank yous as we walked out of the park toward the waiting limo, then headed back home.

Chapter 11

Too soon

The days have been flying by because we are packing as much into them as we can, doing the things Carson loves with him. Sad to say though that none of the things we used to do for fun with Carson are as much fun as they used to be.

Day by day, the pain is getting worse, and he is having more bad days than good ones. Carson has become run down to the point where he has to sleep almost all day long. His stamina started declining pretty fast around the time he started to get different colored tissue and tumors in weird places around his body.

***

My mom and dad are getting married tomorrow, and we are all hoping Carson will be able to enjoy the day. The wedding is going to take place at a plaza about fifteen minutes away from my mom's house. My mom and dad have pretty much fallen in love all over again and all of us couldn't be happier. I will be the maid of honor. Casey will be the best man, and Carson will be the ring bearer. Most ring bearers are younger, but Carson insisted on being the ring bearer, so that is what he will be.

I'm excited about what the future holds because finally, our family is together again, but for how long?

Tomorrow is the big day, and were all ready for it.

Chapter 12

While it lasts

Mom was looking more beautiful than ever. Dad was handsome as ever, and I have to say all of us kids looked great too. I was very nervous on Mom and Dad's wedding day, but not over walking down the aisle at the start of the ceremony.

Mom squeezed into her beautiful white Cinderella dress, and I hooked arms with Casey. After watching our cousins, the other bridesmaids, and the other groomsmen walk down the aisle it was me and Casey's turn. Dad stood at the alter in front of a beautiful field and waterfall. He started to tear up as he watched me and Casey walk down the aisle towards him. He whispered, "You guys look great," as we went to our respective sides of the alter.

Once we took our places, the tone of the event changed. Soft music played as Grandma wheeled Carson up to the alter then sat down. He was carrying the pillow with the rings. Then came the time we were all waiting for. The wedding march began playing, and Mom started to walk down the aisle with grandpa taking her arm.

Dad then fell apart. Cutest thing ever! All of us kids were crying too. I do not know if it was over happiness or how great Mom looks, but we weren't the only ones crying.

About one-hundred-fifty out of the two-hundred guests at the wedding started to tear up too as they watched my mom come down the aisle. The vows and talking about the meaning behind a wedding are usually the most boring part of the wedding, but this time something was different. Carson was brought up to the center, and that my friend is when I fell apart. Carson was handed blue sand, his favorite color. Mom was handed pink sand and Dad was handed green sand. Together, they dumped the sand into a glass vase in the shape of a cross. The cross was then lit on fire on all sides so the sand could melt together. It was the most beautiful thing I had ever seen. There was not a dry eye in the room when the time came for Mom and Dad to say their vows.

"Do you, Joe, take Carrie to be your lawful wife? For better for worse, for richer or poorer, in sickness and in health?" asked the priest.

"I sure do!" said Dad.

"And do you, Carrie, take Joe to be your lawful husband? For better for worse, for richer or poorer, in sickness and in health?"

"Yes please," said Mom, smiling.

"Then by the power vested in me by the State of Florida, I now pronounce you husband and wife—again. Mr. Anderson, you may kiss your bride!"

I swear that kiss lasted ten minutes, maybe more. The whole time, the two-hundred or so people who had attended the ceremony were shouting and cheering and clapping. Carson held his hands tightly over his ears to try and quiet the noise.

After the kiss ended, the groomsmen and bridesmaids locked arms and walked back down the aisle. Every couple had to do a little dance at the beginning of the walk. It was Mom's idea.

When our turn came, me and Casey threw a little duggie at the guests as we continued our walk.

We walked straight from the ceremony to the main hall where dinner was already being served. We sat down to eat some delicious dinner, then it was time for us to dance. Dancing is the best part of a wedding and I know no one can disagree with that! Dancing the night away with Carson, Casey, Mom, and Dad at my side, we had the most fun together we'd had in ages.

When the night came to an end, Mom and Dad stayed at the hotel and Edwin drove home with us kids.

Chapter 13

No more smiles

The day after the wedding we were all sore from the dancing, but Carson was way worse. He could barely walk and when he did it took time and limping. Two days later, Carson was put on bed rest. For those who don't know bed rest is, it is when you are put into bed and will most likely not ever get out.

Carson never smiled again. He was more shy and sad than I had ever seen him before. We had to have a hospital bed installed in his room so it would be easier for him to function, and easier for us to help. Carson just sat in bed all day, playing board game after board game against me and Casey. He wasn't really eating anymore either. He just didn't have the craving for food.

Carson would smile for only for a second, not long enough for any of us to realize that's what he was doing. Nights got longer and more miserable than ever before. My little brother had begun the dying ritual. We all knew he didn't have a lot of time left. The days were just so lonely and different. There were no more smiles and that is not normal for my family, not at all.

A few weeks went by, and as his condition worsened, Carson was put on an oxygen machine. IV's that provided pain medicine around the clock were being pumped into his veins. Never has anything broken my heart more than seeing him slowly wilt away. Carson would just lay there. Half the time, he wouldn't even move all day; but I stayed there in the corner of his room and got him anything he needed.

Meghan and John would sit with Carson too. They had flown into Florida the day before my parents' wedding and decided to stay with us for support until—I can't even say it without starting to cry, so I won't.

Anyway, sometimes John would throw a PlayStation game on the TV and Carson would join in, but not often. The day we've all been dreading is coming too soon and I don't want it to! I am sick to my stomach everyday thinking about the thought of losing him.

The next morning I woke up with only brother alive, Casey.

Chapter 14

What now?

Thursday, the eighteenth of January, I lost someone irreplaceable. Carson went to bed that night and never woke up. Walking into the house that morning, seeing the ambulance and first responders waiting for someone to come out to pronounce my little brother dead, I just sat there. I wasn't crying. I wasn't moving. I sat on the couch in silence as I watched my mom fall into my dad's arms. As Meghan and John hugged me from each side I just stared. I stared out at the ocean.

That night Mom and Dad went to the funeral home with the man who had pronounced Carson dead. They had to plan a funeral for their twelve-year-old son. The devastation in everyone around the house, including Edwin, was insane. No one had any words to say. No one made a sound. The family just sat there in dead silence for the next three days. My mom would try to get my dad, or at least one of us, to eat but none of us had interest. What are we supposed to do next? Does anyone really think you can get over a loss like the one we have suffered overnight? This would take me years to even get over, let alone try not to think about.

I miss him. I miss his light and the energy he gave the family, no matter the situation. The world could be in the process of being destroyed, and Carson would have found something positive about it. That is when I realized that I needed to take over his job and supply the support and energy to my family that they need.

The night before Carson died, when I was putting him to bed, he pulled me forward as he moved his oxygen mask away from his face. He whispered with all the power he had, "I will always love you Carly. I will always be here in Florida. You will find me in the ocean, and my spirit will be in the dolphins. I, Carson James Anderson, will never lose hope."

Carson knew he was leaving us that very night. I believe that is why he said that very thing to me that night. As I talked slowly, but surely with John and Meg, I talked about what we are supposed to do next. The first idea that came to me was that I needed to bring joy back into the lives of my family members again. I needed to do it for Carson.

Meghan helped me get ready, being that I didn't have the energy for it. She curled my hair and put on some makeup, picked me out an outfit, and helped me find some nice shoes. I then ordered two Uber pickups and asked for them to arrive in about an hour. Only four people can fit in each Uber, and there are seven of us, thus the need for two cars.

John, Meg and I headed in to the house as Mom and Dad were packing up their most treasured memories of Carson, like his baby blanket and baby pictures. They placed each item into bins I know they planned to keep forever. We told them to get showered and ready because we are going out.

"Out where?" asked Dad.

"I'm not sure yet, but we're not going to sit around here and cry all day," I said. I was determined to get some smiles and happiness back in this family again.

Chapter 15

Strength

That night we all crawled in the Ubers. Edwin came with me and John and Meghan. We rolled up to Carson's favorite place to eat. It was at the Magic Kingdom, Disney World. You could literally sit in the middle of a hard floor room inside a huge aquarium filled with all different kinds of sea life swimming all around you as you ate.

Carson's connection to the sea is why he loved this restaurant so much. We all got the meal Carson got every time we went there: popcorn shrimp. We talked for what seemed like hours. It was just what we all needed. That conversation was the first step on our respective roads to healing, and we pledged that we were going to do it together…. for Carson.

"Remember the time he took Casey's dry clothes and towel out of the bathroom when Casey was showering?" I asked.

"Yeah, I remember it like it was yesterday," said Casey.

"Me too," said Dad.

Mom frowned, realizing at that moment how much time she had lost with her youngest son. She felt a lot of guilt. Dad picked up on it right away and was there to comfort her. "Carrie, please don't get down on yourself over something you can't do anything about. What's done is done. I just want you to know that Carson loved you very much.

He told me that pretty much every night before he went to bed," said Dad.

"He did?" asked Mom.

"Yes," said Dad, me, Casey and Edwin all at the same time.

Tears rolled down Mom's face as her frown turned into a smile. I was surprised that while talking about Carson, I didn't get emotional. I was smiling the whole time. It actually felt good to smile again. I knew Carson was sitting in the empty chair at the end of the table. I knew he would always be with us no matter what. I knew that if Carson was really in that chair he wouldn't even be able to focus on the dinner because he would be so fascinated by the fish.

The next day was hard, yes, but we celebrated anyway. The next day would've been Carson's thirteenth birthday. He didn't even make the teen stage, which stinks, but he acted like a teenager most of the time anyway. I know Carson is running around in heaven and visiting the sea and dolphins for his birthday. Honestly, I wouldn't have wanted to make him wait any longer. He was in so much pain. He is in a better place now, living a pain free life.

Two days later was Carson's funeral. Attending that somber event was the hardest thing I had ever had to do. Sitting there and listening to people talk about my little brother's short life tore me apart all over again. At the funeral, we family members all sat by the door so we could greet and thank people for coming. All around us were boards filled with pictures of Carson. The photos were from both his time in Minnesota and Florida.

As the room filled up, we are escorted inside, and walked up to the front where a fragile gold vase filled with Carson's ashes was resting on a pedestal. I looked down to see two necklaces and three bracelets. They each had a fingerprint on them. It was Carson's. The girls got the necklaces, the boys got bracelets, and Edwin got one too! The funeral home happened to make these after they took Carson's fingerprint before he was cremated.

No necklace has ever meant this much to me. As my mom put the necklace around my neck, I thought to myself, *I will cherish this forever.* My finger pressed into Carson's print until the priest invited me up to the front of the room to speak.

As I walked up to the podium, I felt my legs shake underneath me. I kept it together until I reached the front of the room and looked back at the blown up picture of Carson smiling. For a moment, I literally froze and felt my stomach tense up. Then I gathered the courage to smile back and start my speech.

"For those of you who don't really know me, I'm Carly Anderson, Carson's big sister. I am nearly five years older, and clearly remember the day he was born," I said. I shared some funny stories about the antics of a little boy who even though he was nearly a teenager never grew up.

"Carson would always be attached to my hip. We had the same laugh, the same taste in food, and the same sense of humor. We were best-friends," I said holding back the tears.

I ended my speech by sharing how much having Carson in my life meant to me. When I was done, I walked over to the blown up picture of Carson smiling, put my hand on top of the picture of his head, and sobbed. "Carson never lost hope, and I Carly Rae Anderson, will also never lose hope." I then took my seat.

The service came to an end a short time later and people filed into the auditorium where the funeral home had prepared cold sandwiches and cookies waiting for the family and friends. As I was munching on my chocolate chip cookie, I looked up to see the most heartbreaking thing of all. Carson's best friend, Jack, was walking straight towards me with tears streaming down his cheeks and what looked like Legos in his hands. He came up to me and set a Lego cross down on the table. He had made the cross just for me.

Jack could hardly get out the words when he said, "C-Carson always talked about you. He loved you so much! "

I reached over and hugged him and said, "I know. He loved you very much too!" I could feel Jack's legs shaking as I hugged him. I asked Jack if he is okay and he told me, "Yes. It's ju-just that I don't think I'll ever have such a good friend again."

I started to tear up again myself and had to look down at the ground rather into his eyes when I said, "Jack, Carson will always be with you no matter what and even if you only have one friend that is all you need and you still have that." He smiled at me as his mom came up behind him to rest her hand on his shoulder. He gave me one last hug before leaving.

When I stood up and turned around, I saw my mom resting her head on my dad's shoulder. They grinned at me. I smiled and walked out to the hall.

Chapter 16

Healing

After the funeral, Meghan and John came home with us, and we all helped Edwin make dinner. Me, Meghan and Mom grilled the burgers, Edwin deep fried the fries, and Dad, Casey and John piled back into the car and headed to the grocery store to pick up buns.

That night, we laughed, we cried, we smiled, and we grinned; but no matter what emotion we were all dealing with, we dealt with things together, and we were getting better, for Carson.

After dinner the boys went to play PlayStation games. Me, Mom and Meghan headed into Carson's room to pack more stuff into boxes. While we were doing the organizing, we talked. There were no tears. Just laughter and smiles as we all shared memories of every little thing in the room.

"Remember when Carson won this stuffed bear at the State Fair last summer," asked Mom.

"How could I forget? He must have spent fifty dollars on that game that required him to knock the bowling pins down to get it."

"Best fifty dollars I ever spent though. The look of pure delight on his face when he won the game was totally worth it," said Mom.

"What's the story behind that signed baseball?" asked Meghan?

"We really don't know," said Mom. "One day Carson was out on the beach and just found it bobbing around in the waves and brought it inside."

"The name on the ball was Kirby Puckett, who spent his entire twelve-year Major League Baseball (MLB) career as a center fielder for the Minnesota Twins," I said.

"I wonder if the signature was from the real Kirby Puckett," commented Meghan.

"We compared it to something we found online and it looks real, so maybe," I said.

"Wouldn't that be something if it were real? A baseball worth hundreds, maybe thousands of dollars, found bobbing in the ocean!" exclaimed Mom. "Cool things like that were always happening to Carson. Weren't they, Carly?"

"Yeah, I guess so," I answered.

Me and my mom have not gotten along this well in a long time. I loved it so much! It felt so good. I guess you could say this is another "miracle" Carson is responsible for making happen.

The next day me, Meg, and Mom headed out to the nearest ACE Hardware to buy paint brushes, stickers, and paint. We then came home and painted Carson's room a sky blue. When the paint dried, we added dolphin stickers all over the walls. We then hug up all the memories with little typed-up descriptions of the memoires underneath them. We even hung up his baby blankets and stuffed animals.

We turned Carson's room into an historical exhibit we could visit anytime we wanted to be with him and our memories. It was actually a pretty creative idea I thought! I will always be grateful to Meghan for coming up with the idea.

Chapter 17

Leaving

In about two weeks, we will be heading back to Minnesota for the school year. Mom and Dad both decided it would be best for me to finish school in the place I've gone since Pre-K. Casey will be starting his first year of college at The University of Miami in Coral Gables, Florida in the fall. After I finish my last year of school in Minnesota, the whole family will be officially moving out of Minnesota and back to Florida to permanently live.

I've already decided that next year, Casey and I will be attending the same college in Florida. I will be going to school to study marine biology, and the University of Miami has one of the best programs in the world. Ever since I knew what marine biologists do, I have wanted to be one, and now the job will have so much more meaning. It means that I can go work with sea life all day, and I will specifically be working with dolphins so I can spend some quality time with my best friend Carson of course.

I am not totally fond of going back to the gross weather in Minnesota, but I know I need to go back for my last year and I can't imagine how many people I am going to have to explain Carson's story to. But you know what? That is okay because any happy moment talking about Carson will be a good one. He was always happy, and I am determined to be happy as much as possible in his memory.

Every morning before we left for Minnesota, I went into Carson's room to just look around, and that room never gets old for me. I love everything about it, especially that I helped with it along the way to making it this great. During those two weeks, each day went pretty much the same way. After spending some time alone in Carson's room, I'd join everyone for breakfast, then we'd spend the day surfing. It was a great way to keep our minds off things and be closer to Carson. After all, he said we would find him in the sea, so that is where we will be!

Four days away from leaving and I was savoring every second of it, from the dances in the park to the shopping trips and sand in-between my toes.

Chapter 18

Not ready

Three days before leaving, I was in my room packing things up with John and Meg's help. My mom came out to the yurt to talk to us. "I just found out that Hope, the dolphin Carter swam with at Discovery Cove, died two days after he did," she said.

"That's an uncanny coincidence," said John.

"That's what I thought at first too," said Mom, "but the woman at the park said that the day Carson died, Hope the dolphin had started acting funny with no warning at all. When I told her about Carson, she explained that dolphins can sense sickness and sadness in people, in much the same way cats can sense fear in humans. She said that dolphins have ways of healing and connecting to someone when they feel it is needed, but she said she has never seen something like this and I had no idea what to say."

I just shook my head and looked out to the ocean and smiled as the sun went down. That night me, Meghan, John and Casey sat up talking as long as we could. We went from venting to cuddling. Me with John and Casey with Meghan. Maybe the timing is right for all of us, but particularly for Casey. He has been trying to hook up with Meghan since the second day she and I became friends.

The next morning, we went to the biggest mall in Central Florida. Orlando's Florida Mall has almost two million square feet of retail space and two hundred and fifty shops. It's a little like the Mall of America in Minnesota, only not as big. We shopped and shopped, and probably spent more than we should have, but Mom did say to buy whatever we wanted, and so we did. Our most memorable purchase that day was a huge stuffed dolphin to put in the corner of Carson's room.

After our shopping excursion, we went out to dinner and when we got back to the house we were met with a huge surprise. There were lights strung up on all of the palm trees leading up our driveway. As we all looked at each other in confusion, we came upon a huge crowd. There must have been a couple of hundred people at the house. We got out of the limo and headed inside after giving what seemed like a thousand hugs, many to people we had never met before.

When we came up to Edwin, he threw his hands into the air and said, "Surprise," then hugged us all.

"Now Edwin, what did you go and do?" asked Mom, with a twinkle in her eye.

"Oh I don't know," he said. "I just called and invited a few people over. I thought that a little party was in order so the summer could end on a high note for all of you," he said.

There were so many people there, it seemed like Edwin had invited everyone who lived in the beach town. Several of my and Casey's high school friends were there too. I recognized several of Mom and Dad's friends from out of state, and country, too.

"How did you pull that together in just six hours? I asked Edwin. He smiled, shook his head and said, "If I can teach you how to surf, I can definitely pull this off!"

He threw me a wink as the music started to play and people started heading onto the dance floor in the recreation room overlooking the ocean. John grabbed my hand and pulled me onto the dance floor. Eventually, Mom and Dad showed up, as did Meghan and Casey.

"They look so sweet together," I shouted into John's ear.

"Yeah they do," he said. "Wonder if they'll hook up."

"If they do, it will be a long-distance relationship since Meghan is coming back to Minnesota with us."

"Yeah, but maybe we'll both get into Miami next year," I said.

"Could happen I guess," said John, shrugging his shoulders.

The party was excellent! At one point, we all went down to the beach and splashed around, then came back into the house, grabbed plates of food and nibbled for a while, then went back onto the dance floor to burn off the calories we had just consumed. By three in the morning, every adult was passed out somewhere in the house. We kids stayed up until the wee hours of the morning talking in my yurt until each one of us passed out too.

Chapter 19

Final goodbye

The next morning, we had a huge breakfast magically whipped up by Edwin mostly using leftovers from the night before. After everyone left, my whole family spent the day cleaning the house until it was spotless. Our garbage man is going to hate us the next time he comes. There is so much trash in the garage right now!

Tomorrow, we'll be flying home to Minnesota. The plan is to stay in the apartment until Mom's real estate agent can find a house for us somewhere out on Lake Minnetonka. It won't be the same as living on the ocean, but it sure will be better than living in our tiny Downtown Minneapolis apartment. I hope Mom can put up with it until we find a house.

The worst part about leaving is that we won't see Edwin for a long time. He will be getting a job with a new family as their butler until we return next summer. "I'll still be with you guys in spirit though," said Edwin. "I am after all going to be stopping by the beach house at least once a week to check on things until you return," he said.

The night before we flew out, we all headed out to the beach with Carson's urn in our hands. Mom then handed it to me, and I slowly turned it on its side and sprinkled his ashes onto the shoreline. I watched the waves take his ashes out into the ocean. We saved just a tiny bit to keep in each house, but most went into the ocean. It is what Carson would have wanted after all. He told me I would find him in the ocean after he was gone, and now I know for sure I will.

The next morning, Edwin helped us load our bags into the limo, then Mom locked the front door and we were off. As we started to pull away from the house, I yelled, "Wait! I forgot something!"

The driver stopped the car suddenly. I unbuckled my seat belt, got out, and ran to the backyard, then up the stairs to the yurt. I unlocked the door, then headed over to the table where the Lego cross Jack had made me for me had been left. I grabbed the cross, then relocked the door. As I headed down the steps, I turned around to get one more look at the beautiful ocean. As I stared out at the calm, blue water, the wind blew my hair out of my face. I said out loud, "Thank you Carson for no ordinary summer!"

After saying that, a dolphin jumped clear out of the water into the light of the sunrise, and then splashed back down and disappeared. I smiled and said, "Goodbye Carson. I love you!"

SIGMA'S BOOKSHELF

Sigma's Bookshelf (www.SigmasBookshelf.com) is an independent book publishing company that exclusively publishes the work of teenage authors, who are between the ages of 13 - 19. The company was founded in 2016 by Minnesota teenager Justin M. Anderson, whose first book, *Saving Stripes: A Kitty's Story*, was published when he was 14, and has since sold hundreds of copies.

"I know there are a lot of other teenagers out there who are good writers and deserve to have their work published, but don't have access to the kinds of resources I do. I wanted to help them," he said.

Sigma's Bookshelf is a sponsored project of Springboard for the Arts, a nonprofit arts service organization. Contributions on behalf of Sigma's Bookshelf may be made payable to Springboard for the Arts and are tax deductible to the extent permitted by law. Donations can be made online at www.SigmasBookshelf.com/donate.

www.ingramcontent.com/pod-product-compliance
Lightning Source LLC
Chambersburg PA
CBHW020623120726
47905CB00003B/921